UNICORN COLOURING and MAZE BOOK

LAKE PRESS

◢ LAKE PRESS

Lake Press Pty Ltd
5 Burwood Road
Hawthorn VIC 3122 Australia
www.lakepress.com.au

First published 2019
Printed in China 10 9 8 7 6
LP22 088

CONTENTS

Welcome to the *Unicorn Colouring and Maze Book!*
A maze may be harder than it looks! The aim of a maze
puzzle is to get from one end (labelled 'Start') to the
other (labelled 'Finish') without meeting any obstructions
or walls - known as dead ends. If you meet a wall,
you must turn around or start from the beginning.
Solid lines cannot be crossed. Your task is to find the
best route possible from start to finish.

The level of difficulty for the mazes in this book gradually
increases. Consider timing yourself at the different levels
to see how long it takes and whether your skill improves!

GOOD LUCK!

Level One:
BEGINNER

BEGINNER

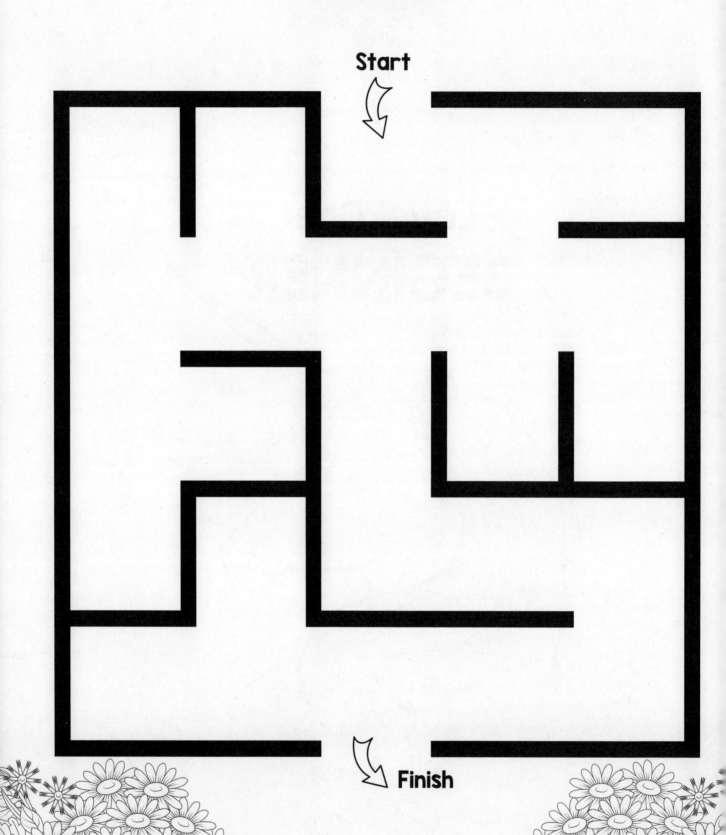

Start

Finish

BEGINNER

Start

Finish

BEGINNER

Start

Finish

BEGINNER

Start

Finish

BEGINNER

Start

Finish

BEGINNER

Start

Finish

BEGINNER

Start

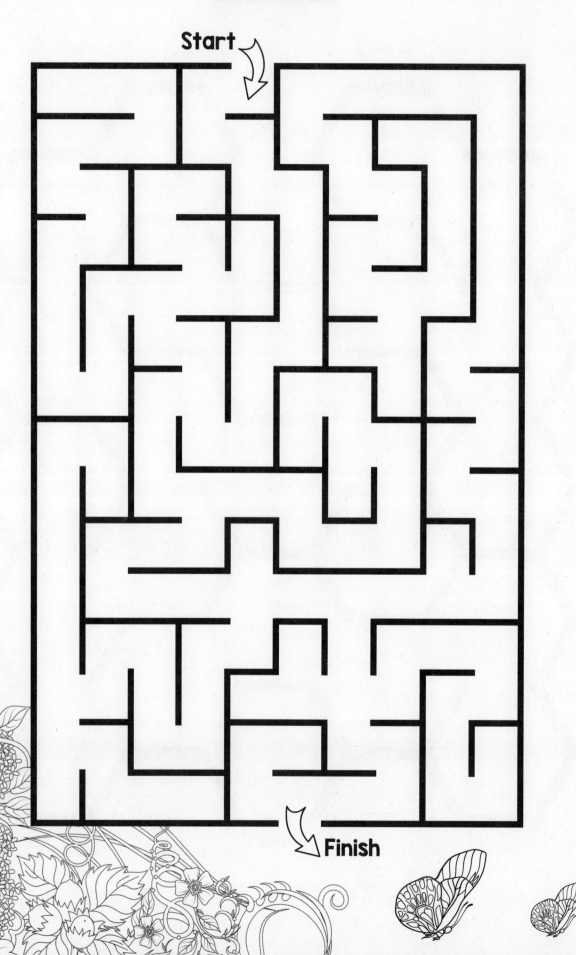

Finish

BEGINNER

Start

Finish

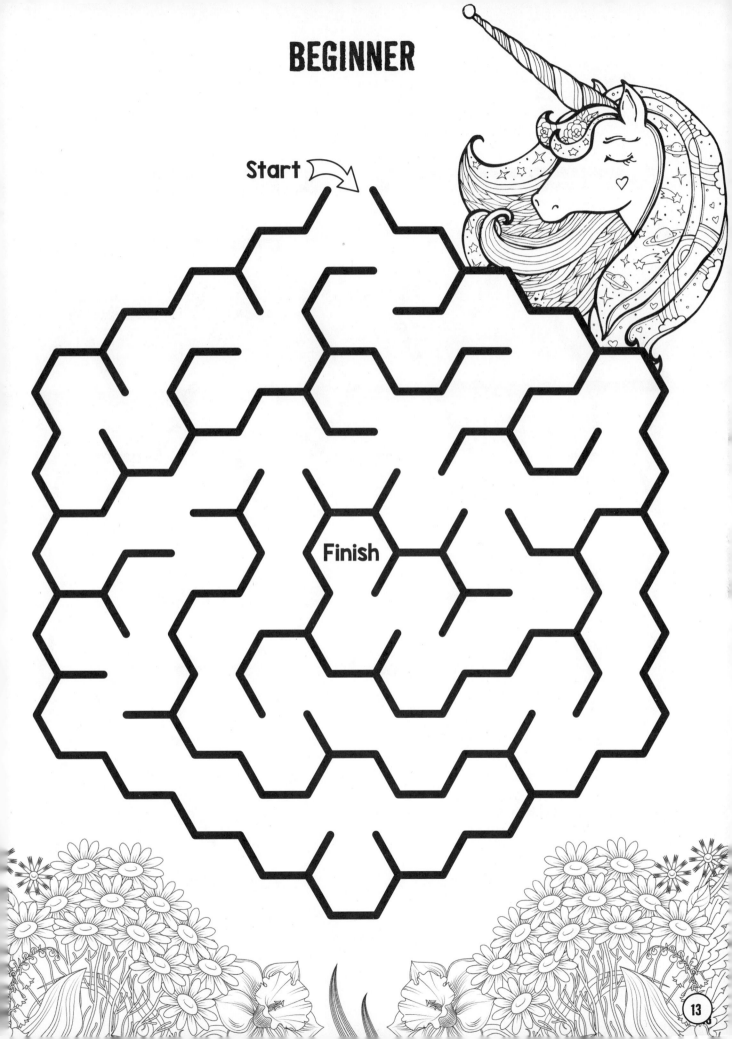

BEGINNER

Start

Finish

Level Two:
INTERMEDIATE

INTERMEDIATE

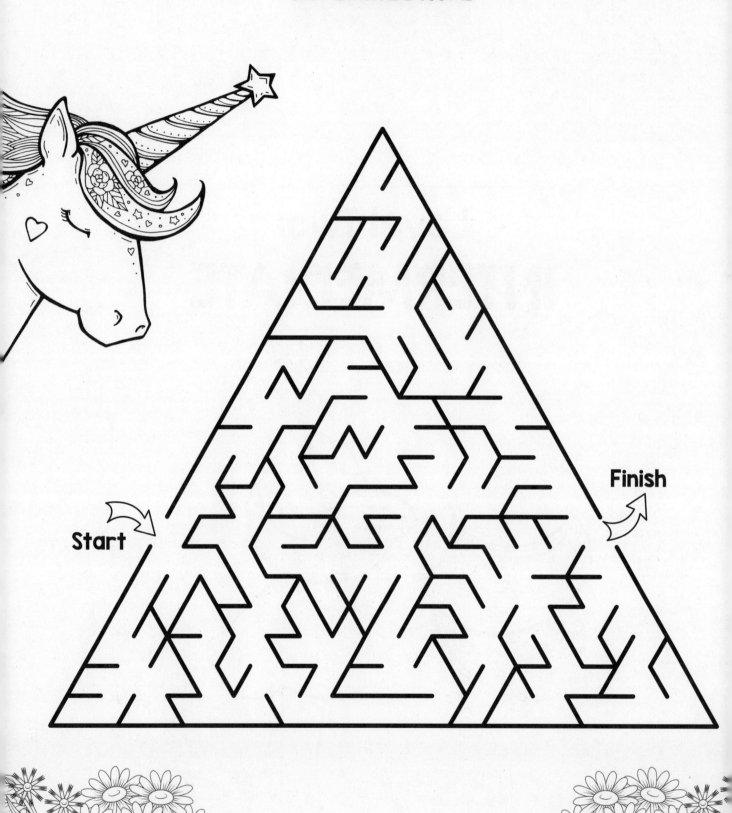

Start

Finish

INTERMEDIATE

Start

Finish

INTERMEDIATE

Start

Finish

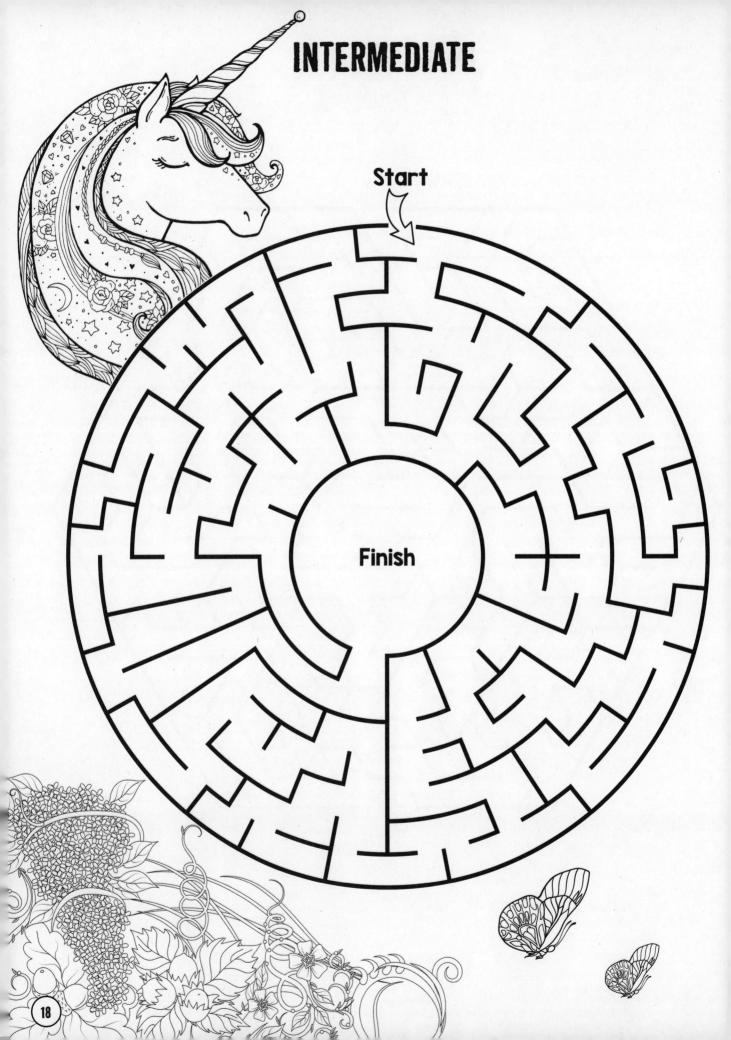

INTERMEDIATE

Start

Finish

INTERMEDIATE

Start

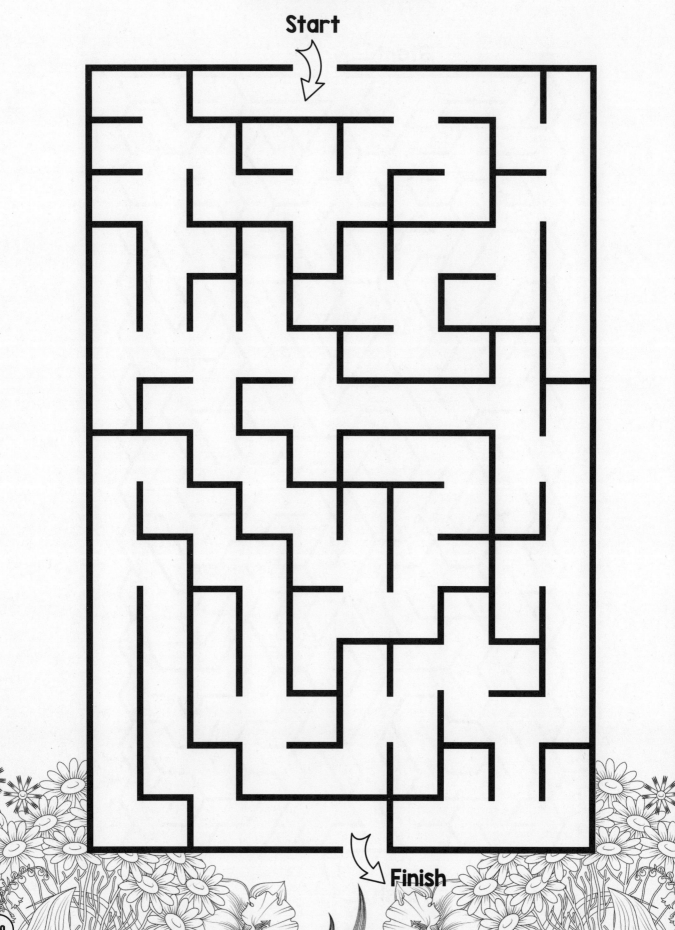

Finish

INTERMEDIATE

Start

Finish

INTERMEDIATE

Start

Finish

INTERMEDIATE

Start

Finish

INTERMEDIATE

Start

Finish

Level Three:
CHALLENGING

CHALLENGING

Start

Finish

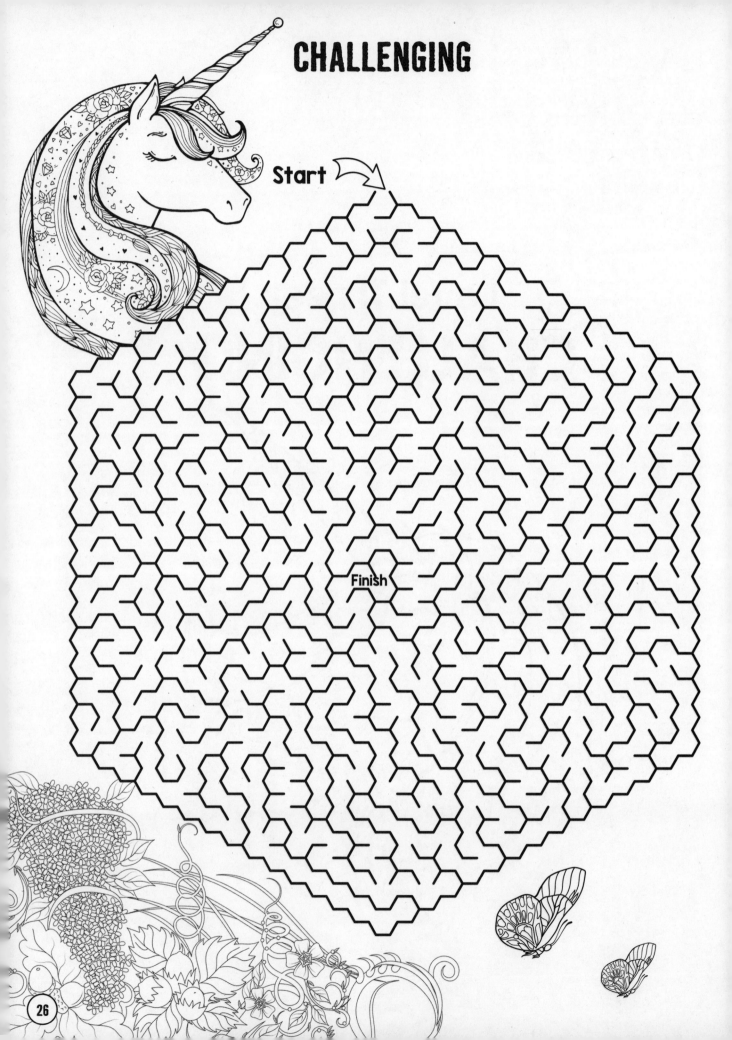

CHALLENGING

Start

Finish

CHALLENGING

Start

Finish

CHALLENGING

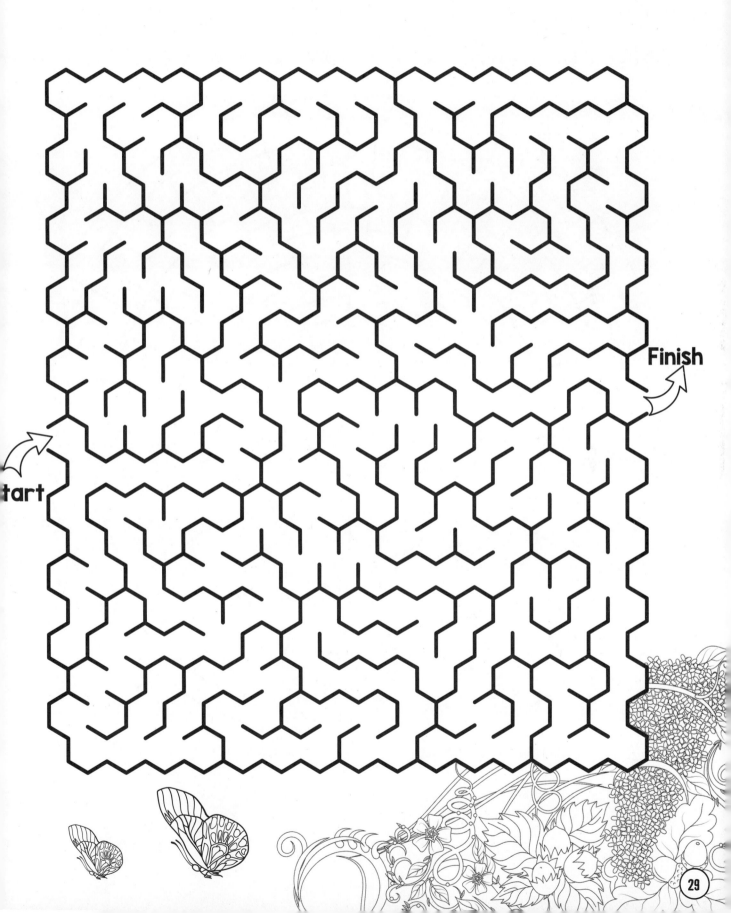

Start

Finish

CHALLENGING

Start

Finish

CHALLENGING

Start

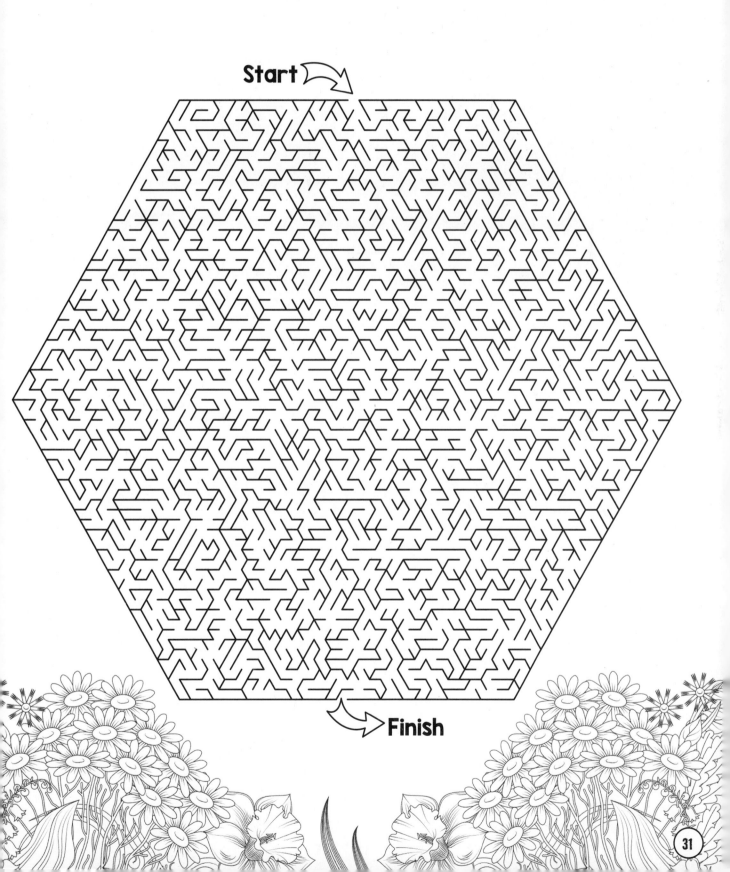

Finish

CHALLENGING

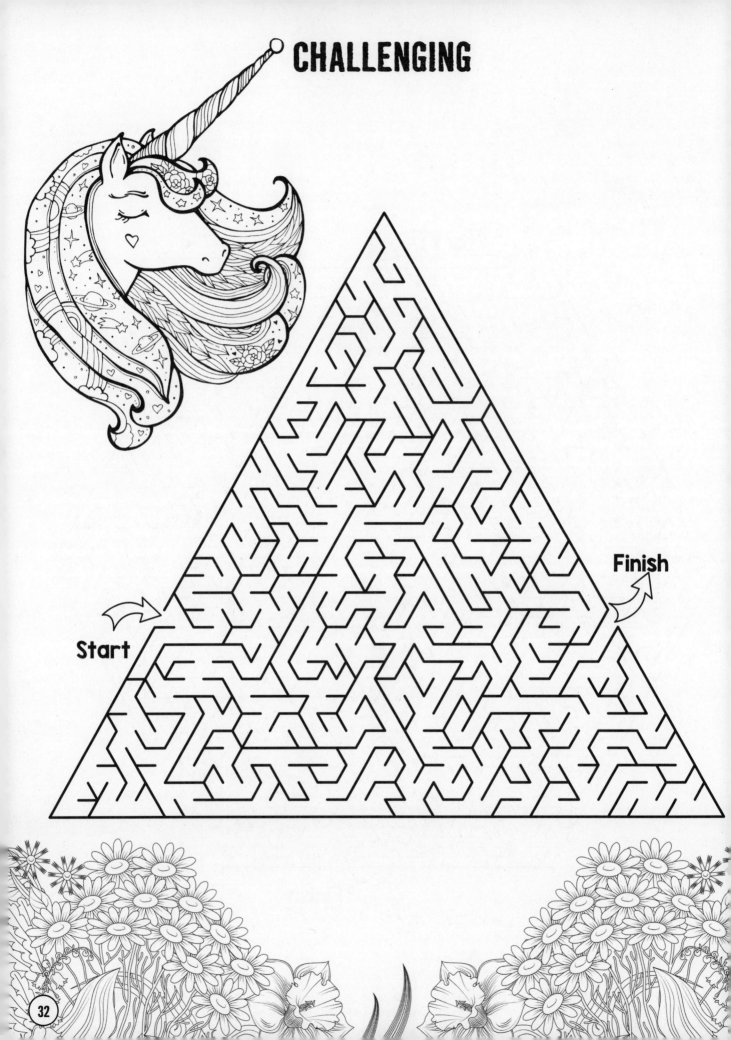

Start

Finish

CHALLENGING

Start

Finish

CHALLENGING

Start

Finish

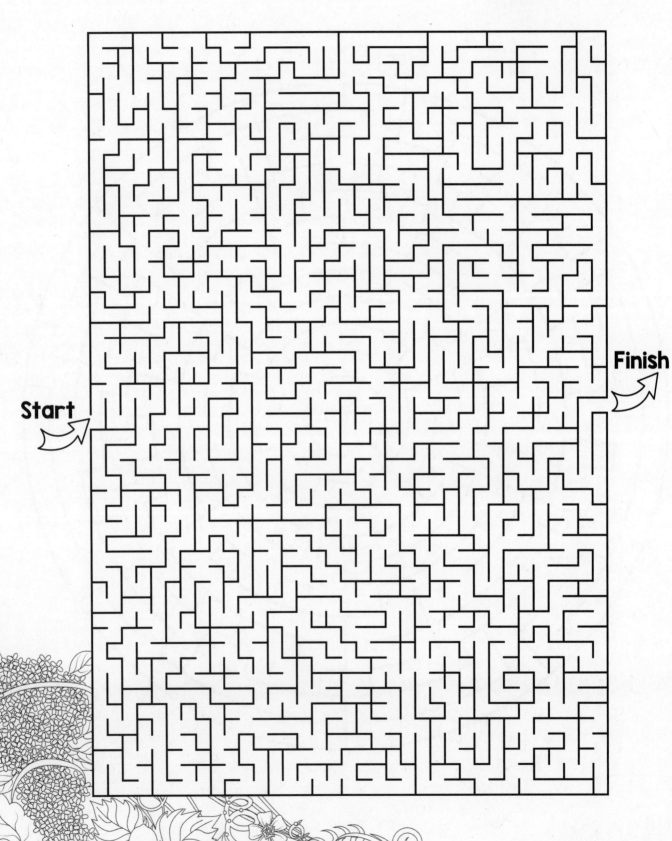

Level Four:
EXPERT

EXPERT

Start

Finish

EXPERT

Start

Finish

EXPERT

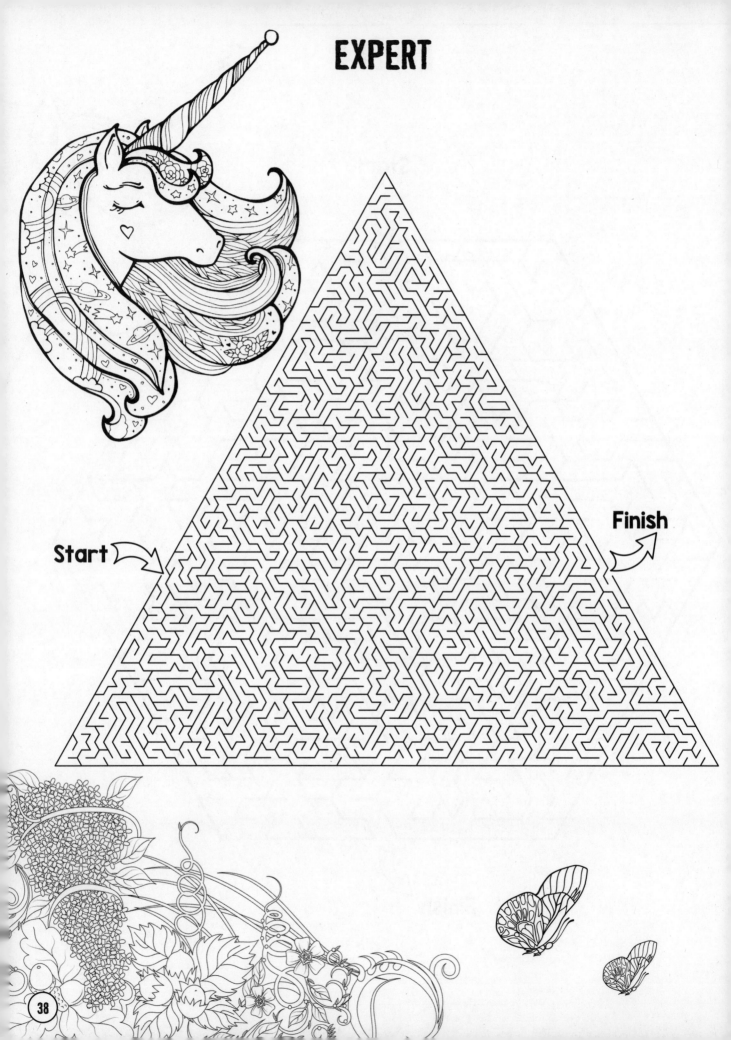

Start

Finish

EXPERT

Start

Finish

EXPERT

Start

Finish

EXPERT

Start

Finish

EXPERT

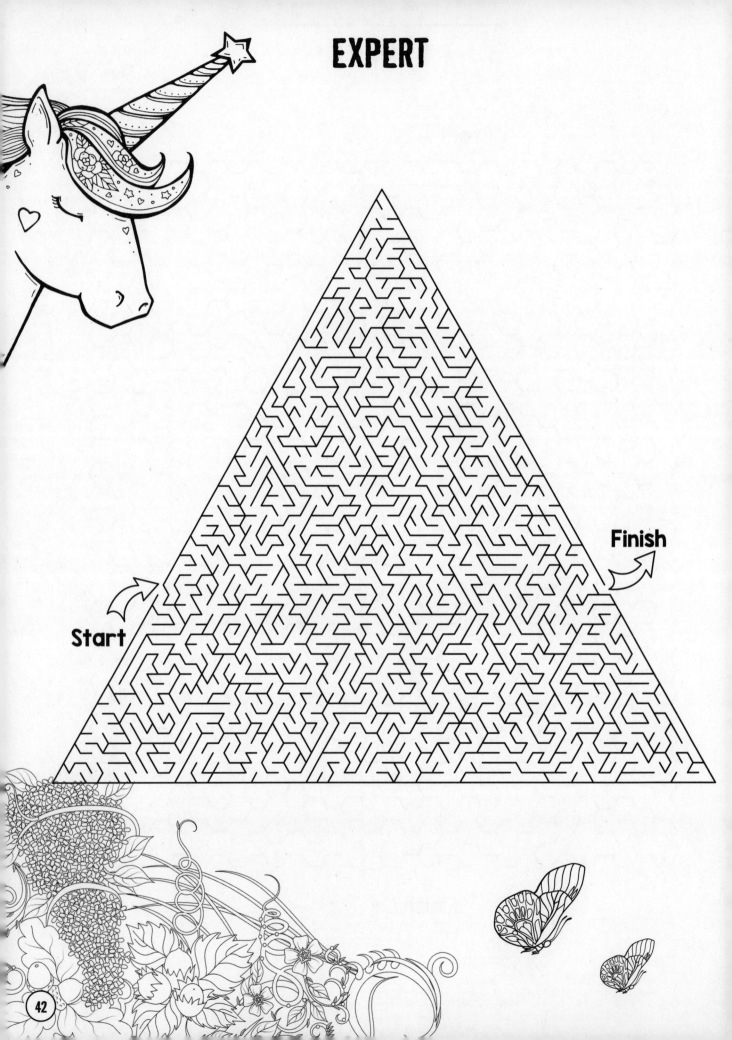

Start

Finish

EXPERT

Start

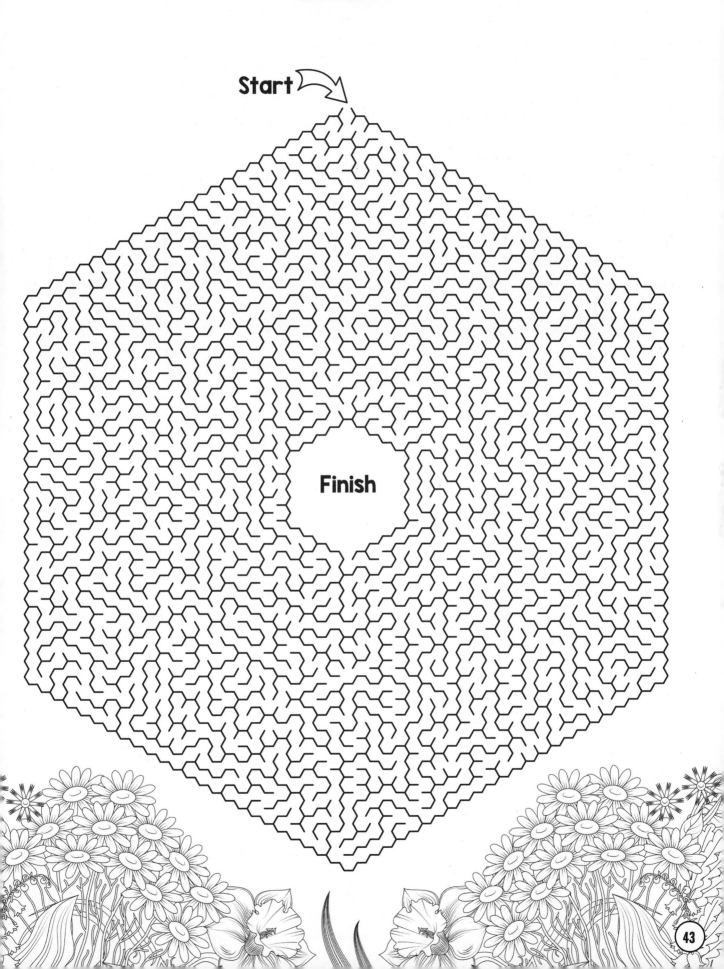

Finish

Page 6

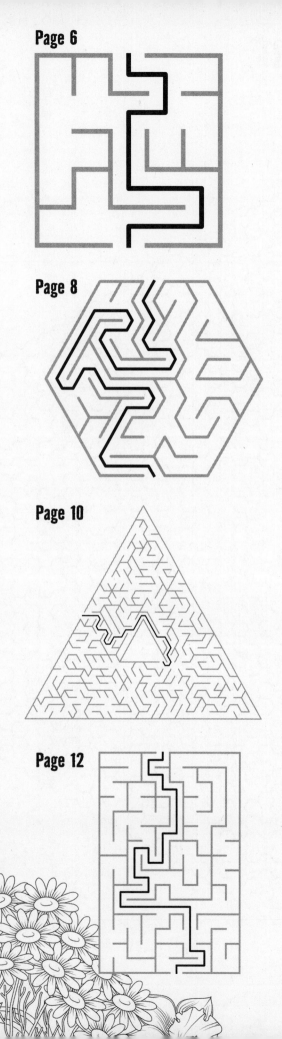

Page 7

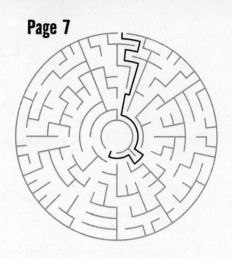

Page 8

Page 9

Page 10

Page 11

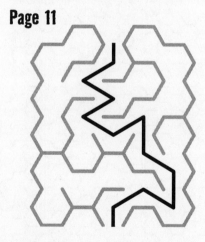

Page 12

Page 13

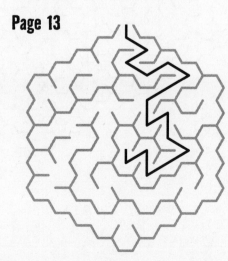

Page 14

Page 16

Page 17

Page 18

Page 19

Page 20

Page 21

Page 22

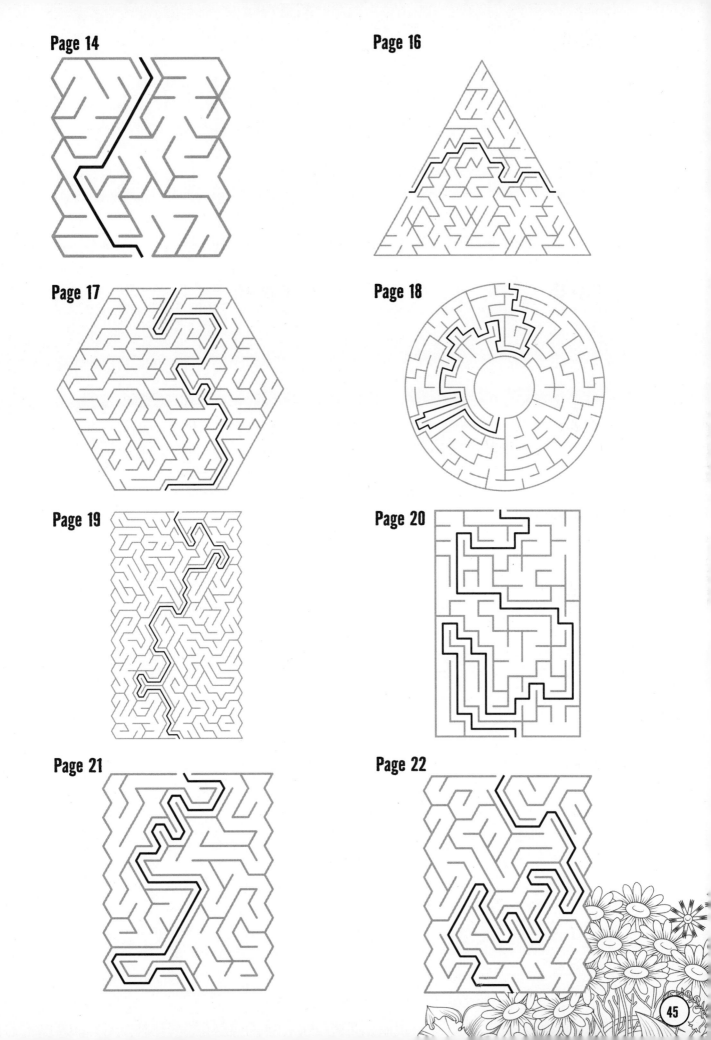

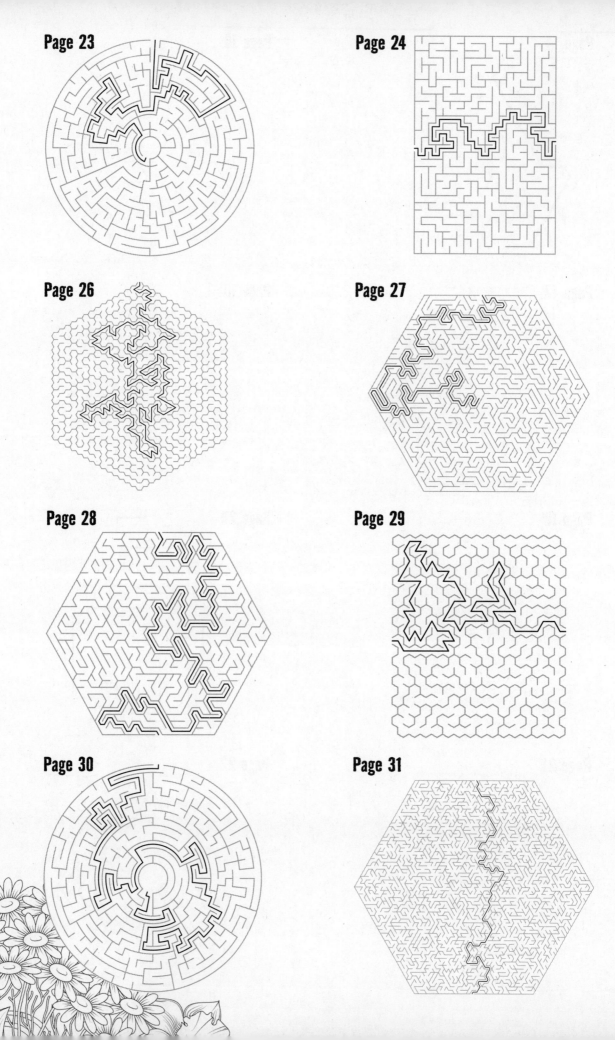

Page 23

Page 24

Page 26

Page 27

Page 28

Page 29

Page 30

Page 31

Page 32

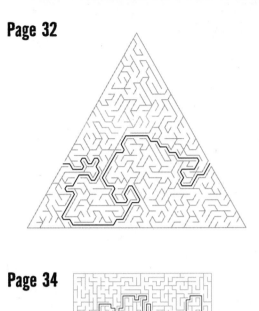

Page 33

Page 34

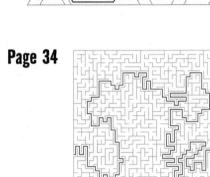

Page 36

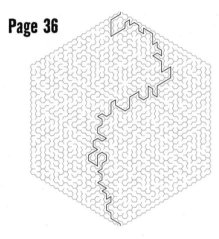

Page 37

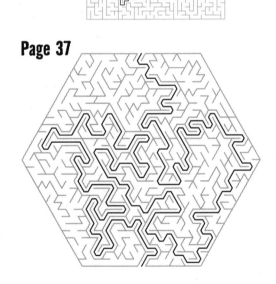

Page 38

Page 39

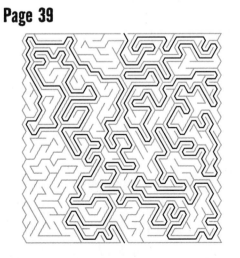

Page 40

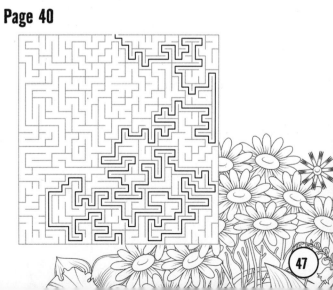

Page 41

Page 42

Page 43

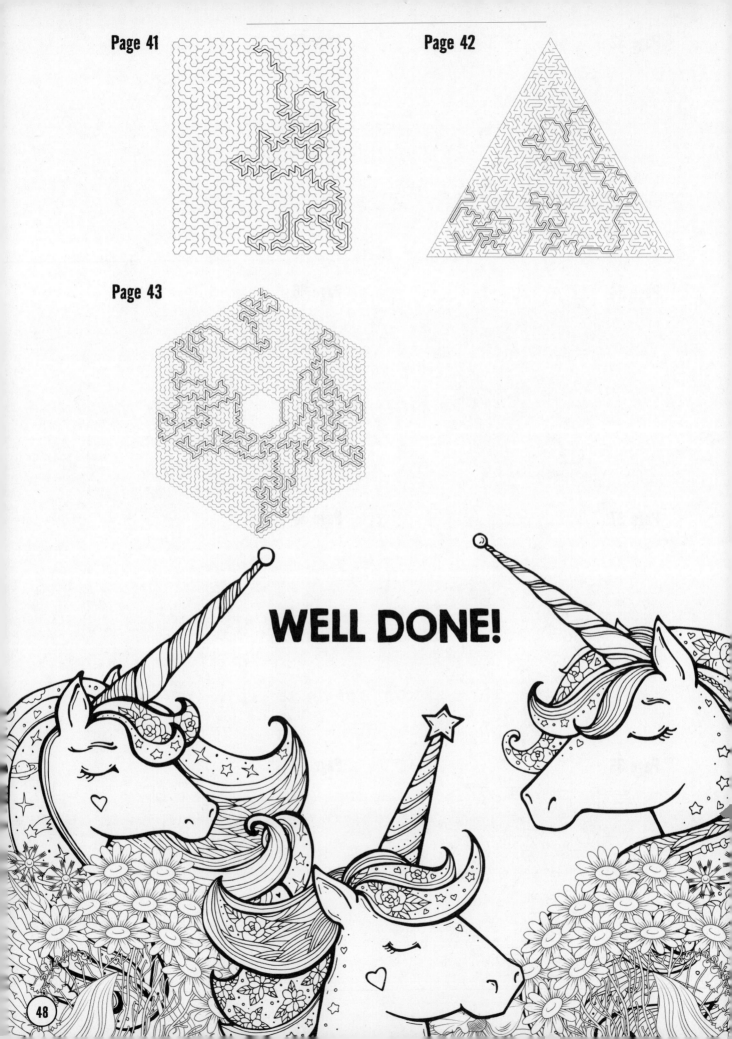

WELL DONE!